DAMSON
the
Donkey

Neil Griffiths

Illustrated by
Janette Louden

Red Robin
BOOKS
Where story matters

For Maxine and Anthony.
Two lovely friends who are dedicated to
giving so many abandoned and unwanted
animals a wonderful life in their home.
(Including a donkey!)

Neil x

Published by

Red Robin Books Ltd

Coppins Barn • Wearne • Langport • Somerset • TA10 0QJ • UK

ISBN: 978-1-908702-27-2

First published in the UK 2017

Text © Neil Griffiths 2017
Illustrations © Janette Louden 2017

The rights of Neil Griffiths and Janette Louden to be identified as
the author and illustrator of this work has been asserted by them
in accordance with the Copyright, Designs and Patents Act 1988.

Design by David Rose

Printed and bound in the UK by Clays Ltd, St. Ives Plc

www.redrobinbooks.com

Contents

Chapter 1
The discovery!

It was a crisp, bright spring morning when Adam first spotted two large ears sticking up above the grass and wild flowers in the orchard. At first he thought it was a hare, or even a fox, but boy were those ears large!

"Perhaps it's a stray dog or could it be Sally their sheep?" he thought. No, she was in the back barn so it couldn't be her. He called Noah, his younger brother, to come and have a look and bring his binoculars. Noah said it was a deer, but as they both weren't sure, they decided to go and take a closer look. They quickly dressed, and Poppy, who was reading her latest book, decided to join them.

As the children lived on a small farm, they were all experts on creeping up on animals, as they regularly had to sneak up on Sally,

their naughtiest sheep, or Peggy, one of the
Gloucester Old Spot pigs, when they needed
to be caught for the vet. They made their
way through the orchard gate and, just like
hunters in the African savannah, shuffled
on their tummies through the long grass.
But they needn't have done any of this as
the creature they were stalking wasn't a bit
frightened and had no intention of taking off.
When they finally reached it, they found a

contented little donkey underneath a damson tree nibbling the odd mouthful of grass. It was the children who looked shocked, not the donkey. In fact, it was if it was saying it was about time and asking what had taken them so long. It actually seemed to be expecting them!

"Where has it come from?" asked Poppy.

"Who knows?" replied Adam. "And, anyway, how did it get into the orchard? The gate's shut."

Noah, who regularly said the first thing that came into his head, announced, "Jesus sent it!"

To start with, the other two laughed uncontrollably, but stopped when they thought he might be right and then started again when they realised how crazy that idea was.

"Where's the mother?" asked Poppy. "It can't be here on its own."

"Well, it's not a baby donkey. It looks about a year old," said Adam.

They searched the orchard, anyway, from top to bottom, then the lower and upper barn and the two meadows at the back of the cottage. Nothing could be found, only their collection of chickens, turkeys, geese, sheep, pigs, ducks, guinea fowl, rabbits, goat and a cow.

"I know!" cried Adam. "Mum and Dad have bought it as a surprise. We haven't got a donkey and this will make our farmyard collection complete," he decided.

The others agreed that this was a real possibility.

They quickly returned to the cottage and tried to look innocent at breakfast.

"Where have you all been?" enquired Mum.

"Oh, getting fresh air!" said Poppy stupidly.

Adam glared, as they never got fresh air that early and Noah was always a nightmare to get out of bed.

Dad came in from milking Milly, their

Guernsey cow, and Agnes, their British Alpine goat. He was so proud that he had been given what he called 'certification' to drink their milk 'straight from the animal'. The children had no idea what that meant, but loved that milk on their cereal, especially in winter, was lovely and warm.

Mum and Dad had worked so hard to set up their smallholding with their collection of animals. They also grew lots of vegetables and sold eggs, the odd piglet, turkeys for Christmas and fruit from the orchard in summer and autumn. Dad was also a music composer and wrote tunes for adverts, and the occasional folk song. Mum wrote children's books and had been published several times.

It was Adam who took courage and asked the first question.

"Well, Dad, how's the farm going?"

Dad thought this was an odd question, but replied politely, "Fine, thank you, but Agnes was a bit grumpy this morning."

"Have you thought about getting any more

animals?" Poppy then asked.

"Not likely. We have more than enough on our hands. But I might buy a few more chickens as some have stopped laying."

Then good old Noah blurted it out. "What about a donkey?" Adam and Poppy glared at him.

"No, we are not. This is a farm, not a pet shop," interrupted Mum firmly.

"Yes, who would want a donkey? They don't do anything," added Dad, "so get that idea out of your heads."

The children ate the rest of their breakfast, more confused than ever. Just where had the donkey come from and, more importantly, how were they going to find out?

Chapter 2

Damson

Having eaten breakfast at top speed, the children rushed back to the orchard. The donkey was now grazing at the bottom near the stream. It took almost no notice of them as they hurtled down the hill towards it.

"Try and stroke it," ordered Adam, who was clearly too nervous to do it himself.

"No, *you* do it," snapped Noah.

"Oh, for goodness' sake, *I'll* do it," Poppy moaned. She was usually the most confident with animals. (But even *she* was a little nervous this time.)

She walked towards the young donkey and softly stroked its neck. Then she patted its side. Eventually, the donkey stopped grazing and nuzzled Poppy as if to say "Go on, keep going."

Now Adam suddenly felt brave and he too began stroking the donkey's ears. It clearly

loved it and soon all three children were
gently hugging and cuddling a very happy
donkey. Under the chin seemed a favourite
spot as it kept lifting its head so Noah could
reach it. If they stopped, it would nuzzle the
children to encourage them to start again!

"Is it a boy or a girl?" Noah suddenly asked.

"I don't know, go on, look," replied Poppy.

"No, *you* look," whined Noah, who was
going red.

"For goodness' sake, *I'll* do it," said Adam (with that voice which seemed to say "I am the oldest, leave it to me!").

This was a job Dad usually did when buying new animals from the market, but Adam thought he now knew enough about animals to determine if it was a boy or a girl.

One quick look under the donkey's tummy and he confidently announced, "It's a girl."

"Aah," they all went in soppy voices, but they didn't quite know why.

"What shall we call her?" asked Poppy.

They all had a think. Then a whole string of names came pouring out.

Dixie – too much like a seaside donkey

Dolly – too sickly

Petunia – too flowery

Clarabelle – too fancy

Dynamite – too ridiculous

Then, to everyone's surprise, Noah offered the name Damson. "Because that's where we found her," he announced, "under a damson tree."

There was silence, as even Noah had surprised himself by having such a brilliant idea.

"Yes, perfect," said Poppy encouragingly. "You clever thing," she added.

And so it was that the new young animal was to be known as Damson the donkey.

The children spent most of that Saturday with her, only returning to the house for lunch. When Mum asked them what they had been up to, they all replied, "Just playing."

It was Poppy who was the first to speak about the situation. "Mum and Dad will never let us keep her. You heard them at breakfast," she sighed.

"But they've got to. She loves us and we love her," snapped Noah.

"We'll have to hide her," declared Poppy.

"Yes, she can be our secret pet," agreed Noah.

But Adam had that 'older brother look' again.

You could just tell he was about to be annoyingly sensible. So, as expected, he asked responsible questions that no one wanted to hear. In fact, he began to sound just like Mum and Dad.

"But she isn't ours to keep. Who really owns her? They must be worried that she's missing. And what about her mother? We don't know how to look after a donkey. Does she still need milk? Anyway, we can't hide a donkey. Mum and Dad are bound to find her. Think of the trouble we'll be in."

These questions made Noah and Poppy really angry inside, but they knew he was right. Noah started to sniffle.

"But I want to keep her," he mumbled.

After a lot of arguing and discussing, the children knew deep down they would just have to tell their parents. So they headed indoors to confess to their discovery with the faint hope that they might be able to keep Damson.

Chapter 3
Hopes dashed

Having confessed, the children were
bombarded with questions from their parents.

"How long has she been there?"

"Why didn't you tell us earlier?"

"You didn't let her in, did you?"

"She doesn't belong to one of your friends,
does she?"

The children explained their story and
Mum and Dad could see they were telling the
truth. Noah started to sob and this seemed to
stop them getting cross.

"Now, now," comforted Mum, "don't get
upset. We'll sort it out."

This made the children begin to feel that
they might actually be able to keep Damson.
But all their hopes were dashed in one go
when Dad turned on his computer, clicked on
Google and typed in 'RSPCA'.

Before they knew it, he had found their contact details and was on the phone to the local office.

The children sat glumly on the sofa. Their ears pricked up when they heard the word 'Police'.

After several other phone calls, which did include one to the police station, Dad returned with just the news the children had longed for.

"Well, no one has reported a missing donkey."

"Yes!" they all cried at the same time.

"But I now have to contact the Donkey Sanctuary in the South West as they may have some information. So don't think we're keeping her," he reminded them.

The children spent the rest of the day watching Damson from Poppy's bedroom window. She kept looking at them too, with the cutest face you have ever seen. There were times she even seemed to be showing off by prancing in the long grass and then rolling onto her back and showing her light furry tummy. This only added to the children's sadness.

Around three o'clock, a dark green van drew up at the front of the cottage and a grey-haired man wearing a tweed cap and jacket climbed out.

"Well, he hasn't come with a horse box, so he isn't going to take her away today," said Poppy optimistically.

This didn't really make the other two children feel any better.

Eventually, the man emerged from the front door with Dad and they headed out to the field. This brought about an instant change in Damson. As soon as she saw them, she bolted off to the bottom end of the orchard and hid behind a large apple tree. No matter how hard they tried, they just could not get close to her.

"She's scared of them," said Adam. "We need to do something."

This was one of those moments when Poppy and Noah tingled with pride for their older brother. All three shot down the stairs and headed towards the orchard. As soon as Damson saw them, she galloped up the hill and stopped right in front of them (much to Dad's relief). The children immediately hugged and patted her. They could feel her heart beating widely and see the heat steaming from her fur. She was snorting rapidly from her nostrils as the children tried to calm her by telling her gently, "It's okay. No one's going to hurt you."

Dad and the grey-haired man stood in total shock and amazement.

"Well," declared Dad, "if I hadn't seen it with my own eyes!"

"You certainly have a way with that little donkey," added the grey-haired man.

Dad told the children that the man was
Mr Jackson from the donkey sanctuary.

Now that Damson was settled, Mr Jackson
checked her over. He looked at her feet, coat,
and even her teeth. He told Dad that she was
in excellent condition and about a year old.
He then brought a microchip reader out of
his pocket, but no chip was found on her. He

said she would no longer need to be with her mother, as she would have stopped taking milk at about six months at the latest. He also told Dad and the children that no one had reported a donkey missing to the sanctuary and he knew no one who kept donkeys in the local area. The children's hearts began to beat faster and hopes of keeping Damson began to rise. He said that the sanctuary was fairly full at the moment, with over 200 donkeys living there or waiting to be fostered. Hopes rose even higher. However, if the family could help by keeping her for a week or so, he would do his best to find her a home. Hopes were dashed. Or were they?

Adam whispered to Poppy and Noah, "If we show Mum and Dad we're excellent donkey carers, perhaps we'll be allowed to keep her."

From that moment on, the children had one mission in life, to become donkey experts!

Chapter 4
Friends

"Thank goodness for Google," declared Poppy.

"And other search engines," added Adam, jokingly sounding like someone on TV who isn't allowed to advertise a product.

A day of research from early in the morning to late at night paid off and the children had a mass of information. As they found out things, they noted them down and, because Poppy had the best handwriting, she wrote out what they called

Our Guide on how to take care of a Donkey, authors Poppy, Adam and Noah Greenwood.

Mum and Dad were in the front room watching TV as the children paraded in holding their report. Both had to admit that they were impressed with the children's work and determination.

The children swaggered with satisfaction. "But remember, a week at the most, then she'll have to go to another home," said Dad.

"Not if we can help it," the children thought.

They really had found out so much.

- A donkey needs at least half an acre of grazing land. (The orchard was perfect.)
- They need hardstanding and a shelter as their coats are not waterproof. (The lower barn was just what was needed.)
- The main food for a donkey is grass, but not too rich, and also hay or barley straw. (The orchard grass was just right and the barn was full of hay and straw.)
- Donkeys need fresh clean water. (There was a trough near the gate.)

- Donkeys are often playful and enjoy rolling and nibbling logs and plastic buckets. (There were already logs that Dad had cut down from old apple trees, and buckets were everywhere on the farm.)
The list went on, but one piece of information worried the children.
- Donkeys are friendly animals and get sad when left alone. They need company.

They knew that they had to go to school and Mum and Dad were always so busy.

"It'll have to be one of the other animals," declared Adam.

"Which one?" added Noah.

They went through the list of animals on
the farm. The chickens, geese, turkeys, guinea
fowl and ducks were instantly eliminated as
they wandered freely all over the farm and
were not particularly friendly. The rabbits
were also off the list as they spent most of the
time hopping around their large outdoor pens
or inside their hutches. It was a bit muddy in
the pig pens and Agnes the goat was always
a grump. So that left the small flock of sheep
and Milly the cow.

Adam, Poppy and Noah made their way
to the lower field and herded the sheep and
Milly into the orchard. Damson watched
closely from near the trough, but made no
effort to come closer and meet her possible
new friends. The children closed the gate
and waited and waited. After what seemed
like hours, they got cold so went inside and
watched from there. It was as if the animals
were ignoring each other.

The children got on with their homework.
Adam had to do a project on the Romans,
looking at uniforms and clothing. Poppy had
to do multiplication questions and Noah
had to practise for his spelling test with really
hard words like 'Autumn', 'tomorrow' and
'February'! When the children finished, they
were to be in for a surprise. When they looked
out the window, there was Agnes the goat and
Damson nuzzling each other over the fence.

"Well, would you believe it?" said Adam. "That grumpy goat has actually found a friend at last!"

They rushed outside and opened the gate to let Agnes in. Damson trotted up to greet her. It was as if they were long-lost friends. They wandered off together and from that day remained regular companions. If one had to leave the orchard for some reason, the other would always be waiting by the gate for their return. Even more surprising, the geese, who were without doubt the scariest animals on the farm and regularly chased visitors, also spent most of their time in the orchard and were brave enough to waddle between Damson's and Agnes's legs!

Well, for whatever reason, the children had now found the friends that Damson needed, so all was going well on the 'what donkeys need' front!

Chapter 5
A new pupil

The following day, Mum drove the children the short distance to their local village school, Green Acre Primary. As the car passed the orchard gate, the children waved from the car and Damson's ears pricked up and she trotted along the fence as if following them on their way.

At school, children were streaming into the playground. Trying to park was as big a nightmare as ever and Mr Ovens the caretaker was directing the traffic as best he could to make sure everyone was safe. Mrs Dodds the lollipop lady was bravely holding up traffic and ushering children across the road like a mother hen. Mr Milner the headteacher was at the front of the school chatting to parents and children. He liked to do this and the pupils loved it when he said hello.

The three Greenwood children couldn't wait for assembly to end as they had so much to say in 'show and tell', but Mr Milner seemed to take ages talking about new beginnings and the joy of spring, showing some tulips and daffodils. Finally, they got to their classrooms. Adam and Poppy were in the same class as they were only a year apart in age. Their teacher, Miss Langley, was only in her second year of teaching and the children adored her. You could tell she loved her job and Mum had said she was always in school on a Saturday working. (Mum knew as she was a school governor.) Their classroom was always full of new and fascinating things. At the moment they had Painted Lady butterfly caterpillars growing and an incubator with six duck eggs inside waiting to hatch. Miss Langley said they were Aylesbury ducks and would take around 28 days to hatch. They were on day 20, so things were getting close. Every day, the children looked for signs of movement. Adam and

Poppy's Dad had said he would take the ducks when they were old enough so they could live happily free-range on the family's smallholding.

The class settled on the carpet and even before Miss Langley had a chance to speak, Adam and Poppy had their hands up straining to share their news. She had no option but to let them go first. The trouble was they both spoke at once and no one understood a word they were saying.

Finally, Poppy was asked to go first (much to the annoyance of Adam). But no sooner had she started, she stopped and just stood there open-mouthed. Adam was staring towards the window too, as peeping above the window frame were two ears. Two ears they knew only too well. But it couldn't be! It wasn't possible! No way could she have got out!

But sudden screams from the playground confirmed their worst fears. The children, followed by the rest of the class, rushed to the window to witness Mrs Dodds being chased around the playground by not only Damson, but Agnes too.

The more she tried to bat them off with her lollipop sign, the more they chased her. Then Mr Ovens the caretaker tried to rescue her, but got butted twice in the bottom by Agnes! Before long, every class was watching the spectacle through any window or door they could find.

RUBBISH

Mr Floyd from the village shop, who had seen what was happening, rushed over to help like a knight in shining armour, but quickly retreated behind the school gate when Agnes charged at him at full speed. Mrs Dodds finally climbed halfway up the school fence and Mr Ovens was on top of a dustbin, shouting, "Shoo!" Knowing that this could all spell disaster, Adam stepped out into the playground, despite Miss Langley telling him to stay indoors.

Thankfully, as soon as Damson saw Adam, she stopped, trotted over and nuzzled up against him. Agnes followed and then began to nibble the flowers in the front tubs.

By the time Mr Milner, who had been called by the school secretary, Mrs Underwood, stormed out, he found two innocent-looking animals, and two terrified adults refusing to move from their positions of safety.

Adam expected the worst and dear Poppy and Noah came from their classes to support their brother. They were ready to 'face the music', as Mum and Dad would often say. They expected to be told off at the very least, but knew it might be:

- Stand by my office and think about your behaviour.
- Write about how you feel your behaviour has affected others.
- Pick up litter for a week.
- Miss a school trip.

But surely it wouldn't be 'suspension'?
All three put on their most angelic faces
that said, "How could you be cross with us?"
To their total surprise, Mr Milner, instead of
being cross, began to smirk, then a full smile

was followed by loud laughing. Soon, laughter could be heard from throughout the school. Even Mr Ovens began to laugh, but Mrs Dodds only managed a slight grin.

After lots of explaining, the two animals were taken onto the school field, largely to stop Agnes eating any more daffodils that probably weren't good for her. There they grazed happily until Dad arrived, towing the animal trailer from home.

Mr Milner spent ages talking to him and the children thought they still might be about to get into trouble. But when the children got into the car, they were greeted with some surprising news.

"Well, I don't know how you three do it, but it looks like Damson might be joining you more often. Mr Milner has had an idea. He wants to set up a school farm and guess who the star guest is going to be?"

Chapter 6
Found!

All the way home the children chatted excitedly. They couldn't believe how what might have turned out to be the worst day ever became one of the best. Dad, however, had other things on his mind. Just how had Agnes and Damson got out?

Once home, the children were sent to inspect every inch of the orchard fence whilst Dad checked both gate latches. There was no damage anywhere and there was no way Agnes and Damson could have jumped the fence as Mum and Dad had invested in an extra high one to deter deer from getting in and nibbling at the fruit trees. So the mystery of where Damson had come from and how she got in and out continued!

After such an exciting day, the children were brought down to earth with a sudden thud. Mum reminded them that they were not keeping Damson forever and that they had promised the man from the donkey sanctuary to do their best to find out if she had been lost locally. For homework, the children were asked to make 'Found' posters to put around the local neighbourhood. They were furious, as they didn't want anyone to find her!

Their first set of posters were put straight into the bin by Mum as the children had deliberately made them too small and used handwriting no one could read!

Adam was even sneakier as he had put the wrong telephone contact at the bottom so no one could reply. Poppy was also crafty as her description of Damson was enough to put anyone off claiming her.

DONKEY FOUND

Dirty in colour
She bites,
kicks and
chases people.

P.S She also
escapes all
the time!

Mum and Dad said, "Creative, but unacceptable." So new posters were reluctantly made.

The children then suggested ridiculous places to put the posters in the hope that no one could see them. Adam suggested one on their front door.

"Who would see that? Even the postman leaves the post in a mail box at the end of our lane," moaned Mum.

Other suggestions such as in the middle of a large roundabout with bushes were also rejected. Finally, Dad took control and went off and put them in the village shop, on the school noticeboard, in the bus shelter and on the church news board. To make the children almost despair, he then contacted the local newspaper and they put a free notice in the Lost and Found section for him.

Over the following days, the children jumped every time the phone rang and their hearts raced whilst waiting to hear bad news. However, they only had calls from Mrs Briggs ordering eggs, and three from their grandma in Southampton.

Thinking that the days spent with Damson might soon be over, the children decided to be with her as much as they could. Thankfully, neither she nor Agnes escaped or came to school again that week, but as soon as the children got home each day, they would head to the orchard. They groomed Damson, cleaned her feet and did lots of patting and cuddling, which she loved. Each night, they took her to the lower barn and filled up the hay net and 'tucked her in'.

At school, they were thrilled that Mr Milner really was serious about having a school farm and Mr Ovens was out on the field every free moment he had constructing a fence around a corner that was rarely used by the children.

Mr Milner had announced the news in assembly, to cheers from the whole school, and asked every class to send him ideas and thoughts. Miss Langley encouraged her class to do lots of research and she put up information about school farms on the interactive whiteboard. One school in Gloucestershire had pygmy goats and another in Bedford had a duck pond. Noah's class sent Mr Milner pictures of what they thought the farm should look like and he decided that a School Farm Committee should be set up with a representative from each of the five classes. Noah was immediately elected by his class as they thought he knew lots about animals. In Miss Langley's class, Adam and Poppy got equal votes and Adam decided Poppy should be the representative as he was already captain of his school house St Andrews and the football team. The committee met with Mr Milner and Mr Ovens, as he was going to make most of the things, and Mrs Harvey the Reception class teacher as she had animals at home. Finally a plan of action was drawn up after sifting through lots of ideas and throwing out the silly ones such as "Can we have a camel?", "Could we have swings for the pigs to play on?" and "Do dinosaurs live on farms?".

At the end of the school day, the children couldn't wait to get home to tell their mum and dad, as they had both promised Mr Milner they would come in and help with the farm too. But as they drove up the drive with Mum, they were faced with a sight they had dreaded. It was Mr Jackson's van with an animal trailer behind it.

Chapter 7
Supermarket dash

The children looked in the orchard as they passed and Damson was nowhere to be seen. "She must already be in the trailer," they thought.

"Don't look," said Adam. "Just follow me to the upper barn," he told them.

By the tone of his voice, Poppy and Noah knew not to argue. Once there, they sat in silence on straw bales listening to Milly the cow chewing in the corner as the older brother Adam broke the silence to say what he thought older brothers should say at a time like this.

"We've got to be brave and not cry," he said.

Well, this immediately made the other two burst into tears. So he started again.

"Damson will go to a good home where they'll love her as much as we do."

That made it even worse and Poppy began to almost howl like a dog.

"We must be glad we had her for nearly a week," he offered.

Then he began to cry too.

"It's not fair," wailed Poppy.

"I'm going to run away and find her and live with her," sobbed a very confused Noah.

"We never get to keep anything," said Adam unfairly, as they already had ten chickens, six sheep, eight ducks, seven turkeys, nine guinea fowl, five pigs, one goat, three rabbits and one cow. Oh, and four geese!

The children went on and on and the crying got louder and louder. In fact, it would probably have gone on all day if they hadn't been silenced by even louder laughing. Well, kind of laughing.

"Shut up, it's not funny," whined Poppy.

"Yes, clear off and leave us alone," mumbled Noah.

It took several seconds before the children realised the noise of laughing was coming from Damson. She was braying for the first time! She was standing in the door of the barn with Mum and Dad who were smiling broadly, either side of her.

"What's up with you lot?" asked Dad.

The children didn't know what to say.

"Well, if that's your attitude, perhaps we should rush after Mr Jackson and tell him to take Damson after all," added Mum.

"What do you mean?" questioned a really confused Adam.

"Well, we've decided to keep Damson as she's going to be needed at the school farm and she's keeping the orchard grass down nicely," said Dad.

"Also Agnes would probably miss her and perhaps you might too?" he asked.

At that moment, the children burst into cheers and wrapped themselves around Damson, Mum and Dad. Even Milly the cow got several cuddles, much to her surprise! They told the children that Mr Jackson hadn't found Damson a new home, but had said he would try and squeeze her into the donkey sanctuary. Mum and Dad hadn't liked that idea even though it was a wonderful place, and had secretly fallen in love with Damson as much as the children had. And so it was that Damson found a new home.

The children simply adored Damson and spent as much time as they could with her. She loved their company and the children learnt more and more about how to care for her. However, one problem continued – she loved to wander and regularly followed the family! It was as if she had a magic way of getting out of the orchard or barn. She also had a dog-like nose that could follow a scent and always find where the family were, which caused some very embarrassing moments.

Perhaps the worst was one Saturday when they were shopping.

"Oh, look," said Noah, "there must be a robber in the supermarket. There's a flashing police car outside the front entrance."

"I bet they've got him handcuffed and pinned to the floor," added Adam.

"Wow, perhaps there are two or three thieves as four more police cars have turned up!" said Poppy.

"I bet they have guns," warned Adam.

Noah hid behind a huge stack of Heinz baked beans.

"Don't be so silly," snapped Mum, even

though she was edging behind the beans too. Then an announcement was made that really did scare them all, even Dad.

"Would all customers remain calm. The situation is under control. Please remain where you are and do not move."

This terrified everyone, but no one moved an inch. They were made to feel worse when they saw staff cowering behind the meat and cheese counters, and one mother had plopped her child into an open-topped freezer compartment but then plucked him out again when he started to turn blue!

Then the ominous tone of a helicopter could be heard hovering overhead and from its loudspeakers the pilot was shouting, "Remain calm, do not enter the supermarket. I repeat. Do not enter the supermarket."

By this time, the three children had crawled under the biscuit shelves and Noah took the opportunity to grab a packet of ginger nuts as rations, just in case they were going to have to stay there for days!

"This looks serious," whispered Adam.

Even Mum and Dad looked frightened, peering from behind the beans. But they were not to stay there for long as in an instant there were shouts of "Take cover" as tins, bottles, boxes and fruit and vegetables came flying over the shelving. The supermarket was filled with sounds of crashing and banging while, from behind a huge tower of cornflake boxes that suddenly collapsed into the coffee and biscuit aisle, the culprit of the whole incident emerged – one little donkey named Damson.

"On no!" gasped Mum. "Pretend we don't know her," she whispered.

But that was quite hard to do as by now the children had emerged from under the shelves and Damson was nuzzling them endlessly. They hadn't the heart to ignore her, especially as she had a carrot stalk dangling out of her mouth and cornflakes all over her coat.

CUSTOMER SERVICE

FROZEN

COFFEE & TEA

Of course the whole episode appeared in the local newspaper and then, to the family's horror, on the national TV news. (The phone went all day at home.)

Dad was forced to go to the police station, but was let off with a caution, not that the children knew what that was. Despite all the commotion, the damage was not as bad as it had first looked, but Mum and Dad had to find £800 to replace the cornflakes and vegetables Damson had eaten and the shelves that had been broken. The whole family helped with the clean-up and the police did have to admit they had perhaps overreacted with five police cars, 21 riot police officers and a helicopter. They said the manager had panicked on the phone and thought a herd of wild animals had invaded the shop. Much to everyone's embarrassment, envelopes of money kept coming through the post from kind people who took pity on the donkey and wanted to help pay the bill. A total of £6,508.44 was donated. All the money was given to Mr Jackson at the donkey sanctuary. He was thrilled with the gift, so some good did come out of a day the family would never forget!

Chapter 8
Breaking in

Similar days were to follow at the swimming pool, hairdresser's and garden centre in the local town, but none were quite as bad as that day at the supermarket! The family had been told that donkeys were great escape artists, but it was still baffling them how Damson kept getting out!

The school farm had really taken off and it now had four hens, two ducks and two sheep. Damson appeared twice weekly as a star guest and Agnes only made it once before being banned. The reason? She ate her way through a flowerbed and swallowed a child's hanky that was dangling over the fence.

"Fortunately, goats have four chambers in their stomachs and can digest it," Mr Milner told the upset children. How he knew that was a mystery!

It was a question from one of Adam's friends that then set the family a challenge.

"Can I ride her?" asked Abby.

"No, you can't ride donkeys," Adam replied abruptly.

"Well, you can at the seaside. I've been on one," she responded.

"That must be a different type," Adam answered pathetically.

"But *could* we ride her?" he began to think.

After lots of discussion, Mum and Dad were finally persuaded to let one of the children just sit on Damson. Just once!

The children, of course, thought they were going to ride Damson the following day, but were horrified to be told it would take weeks, or perhaps even months to train her. It began with lots of patting and cuddling, which Damson loved. They had to make sure she was comfortable being touched. That was not a problem for this donkey as she loved a scratch on the bottom, pat on the neck,

gentle rub on the ears, tickle on the tummy and nuzzle on the nose! Then Dad had to teach her how to lift a hoof. He used lots of commands and rubbing of her legs.

Damson loved all this fuss and the more attention she got, the more she liked it. They had no trouble placing a halter on her and she would happily be led around the farm as it gave her the chance to meet all the other animals. After several weeks of leading, they put a rug on her to get her used to the feel of it. Then Noah had the sweet idea of putting his large teddy on her back as they led her around the orchard. Mum had bought a lightweight saddle made for donkeys, which Damson seemed to like as when they put it on her, she almost paraded along! After several weeks of preparation, Mum and Dad decided Damson might just be ready for someone to sit on her. It was Noah who was chosen to be the first to ride her.

"Why him?" moaned Poppy. "He's too young," she grumbled.

But Dad thought it should be the lightest
child and Noah was good with all the animals
and rarely got frightened. He placed Adam's
riding hat on Noah's head. He gently lifted
him and to start with, Noah just lay on his
tummy across her back. Damson nuzzled his
legs. Then bit by bit, Dad placed him on her
back. No one dared make a move or sound.
But they needn't have worried. Damson let
out a small snort and began to graze. Poppy

then had a try and finally Adam got a go. He had been riding ponies for some time at the Four Oaks Riding School. Dad tied the lead rope around the halter so Adam had his own reins. Damson looked round at him as if to say "About time. Now let's go!"

"You look like a jockey!" shouted Poppy proudly.

"A donkey jockey!" joined in Noah.

Adam beamed and raced faster and faster.

"Wow, that donkey can really motor," said Dad when they finally came to a halt.

"You'd win any race," called out Poppy.

"Yes, even the Grand National," he replied.

Then all at once everyone cried, "The Donkey Derby!"

This was an event that was held every year at the Newton Down Country Show. The family went regularly, and Mum and Dad had won some cups for showing their Gloucester Old Spot pigs. As an annual attraction they had a Donkey Derby. The RSPCA were always there to check the animals were healthy and

Mr Jackson and some of his staff always went
to make sure the donkeys were happy and
well cared for.

"No, it's too dangerous," Mum suddenly
said.

"Yes, not really a sensible idea," added Dad.

"Oh!" the children cried. "Pleeease!" they
whined.

"It's been my dream," announced Adam.

(This was a complete lie as he had only just thought about a Donkey Derby.) But it worked as Mum changed her mind almost instantly.

"We did come and live out here for the children to live life to the full," she said, to everyone's surprise, especially Dad's.

"Okay, but we need lots of practice and if we're going to do it, we do it properly," he said.

"You mean we're going to win!" declared little Noah.

Everyone cheered.

"Yes, we are!" they all thought.

Chapter 9
Crash landing

The weeks that followed seemed to have only one focus. Derby Day! Yes, homework was always done first, and chores around the farm. The children had always been expected to help out and regularly fed the animals and changed the bedding straw in the barns. They also had to check the troughs were clean and fresh and had to take their turn mucking out Milly the cow too! But once all the jobs were done, they would be off into the orchard to exercise Damson.

Their parents had bought a proper donkey bridle and the children were so happy to get it, they cleaned it every day. Sometimes they took Damson up into the top field where they had a much larger space to race. They got quite professional about things, with Poppy in charge of the stopwatch to time Damson's runs and check the reins were on properly. Noah was glad to have little rides in between.

Damson seemed to love all of this and when it was time to go back to the orchard, she would pull on the reins as if to say, "No, don't let's stop yet!"

The children were thrilled when Mum painted Damson's name on the brow band in purple leather paint, the colour of a real damson. It seemed that July 5th would never come, but eventually it did. The day of the Donkey Derby!

Damson was brushed endlessly until she really shone, which wasn't easy for fur! She had her hooves picked out of any mud and then polished with special black polish. She was loaded up in the trailer and brayed loudly to Agnes as if to say, "Won't be long!" But Agnes looked so grumpy at being left behind that Dad had a change of heart and loaded her in too, to keep Damson company.

On the way, Mum handed Adam a package. Inside was a purple and green shirt and a purple hat cover with a peak.

"I made them for you. They're called 'racing silks'. We want you to look the part. A real jockey!" she beamed.

Adam couldn't reply as tears of joy were welling up in his eyes, so he looked out the window to hide his emotions. Mum and all the others knew to say nothing, but felt tears too.

As they arrived at the Country Show, Damson must have heard the music of a brass band playing in the main ring and began to bray loudly. People were streaming into the show, as it was always so popular.

Noah spotted a fun fair through the car window. There was a big wheel, swing boats, a carousel with colourful horses, of course, chair swings and his favourite – the helter-skelter. He then announced the order of rides he would go on. The helter-skelter came first and the chair swing last in case he felt sick. Mum reminded him that no one had said he could go on any ride as they cost £2 a go. His face dropped, but a smile from Mum in the car's rear-view mirror restored his hopes again.

All the animal trailers were directed to parking zone D. The family parked up next to a huge horse box with the words 'Golden Beech Jump Team' on the side in shiny gold letters. There were four beautiful bay horses tethered outside, all wearing navy blue horse blankets, and long yellow socks around their legs. Inside the front of the horse box was actually a seating area where three people were eating breakfast.

"That costs about £230,000 to buy," Dad informed the family.

"What! That's more than a house!" Mum gasped. "Anyway, how do you know what it costs?" she asked.

"Saw it online. One can dream," he sighed.

Dad had wished he had washed their trailer as it looked really grubby next to this shiny monster.

When they brought Damson and Agnes out of the trailer, they could hear sniggers from their 'neighbours'.

"Well, let's just see who wins at the end of the day," Mum said defiantly, towards the 'shiny monster'.

The 'neighbours' just looked on.

The family then decided to take Damson for a good look around the show and put Agnes back in the trailer with lots of hay to keep her happy.

The Country Show was beginning to get into full swing. There were stalls of every

kind – plants, clothes, food, pet treats and even somewhere you could get a massage or your nails painted. Large tents big enough for a circus housed a craft area, flower show, food festival and cookery exhibition. At the far side of the showground were the livestock tents and showing rings. Damson seemed to love meeting Hereford and Ayrshire cows, Tamworth and Oxford Sandy and Black pigs, Herdwick and Jacob sheep and even an alpaca! In fact, she was enjoying every moment and was on her best behaviour. Well, she was until the local hunt and their pack of hounds made their way towards the main ring.

Damson saw red (literally, as the huntsmen and women were wearing red jackets), reared wildly, pulled the rope from Dad's hands and bolted off. She hurtled through the flower tent, causing one woman carrying a large red begonia to faint, and another with a tall ornamental grass to run faster than she ever had before. Damson narrowly missed the floral art displays (this year the theme was Tropical Sunrise) but caught a string of

coconuts on her ears. The noise they made
caused her to panic even more and she
headed through the Army assault course.
There she vaulted poles and weaved around
dangling ropes and finally splashed through
a deep boggy pond. Then she headed across
the show jumping ring, getting a 'clear round',
but not intentionally, and caused chaos in
the Pygmy goat show area before eventually

heading into the main ring where they were
waiting for the landing of the parachute team.

Once in the ring, Damson spotted lush grass so came to a sudden halt and grazed innocently. As eight skydivers began to land, all but one managed to avoid Damson, who took no notice of the thuds as they landed, or their colourful billowing parachutes.

Despite all efforts, one young skydiver landed, thankfully gently, straight onto Damson's back. For a moment she looked slightly stunned, but then settled back to

grazing. The audience, who had initially looked stunned too at seeing a coconut-entangled donkey with a skydiver on its back, thought the whole spectacle was part of the show. They suddenly started clapping and cheering and gave a standing ovation. Even the show's president stood up in the members stand and applauded wildly. The skydivers had never had such a reception so decided to go along with it and any anger from show officials at the mayhem Damson had caused quickly disappeared. She was a hit and a star of the show! The family were shoved into the main ring and forced to take some applause too. They actually began to enjoy it and almost showed off as they led Damson from the ring.

The secretary from the president's tent put a red sash which said 'Newton Down Country Show, Best Exhibit' over Damson's neck as she came out. Throughout the rest of the day, everyone cheered as they passed by and Damson got hundreds of pats, which she

loved. The family also got free hot dogs and ice cream, and one of the pet stalls insisted on giving Damson a free new halter, blanket and hay net in return for a photograph with the new donkey star.

However, Dad reminded the family that the celebrations needed to end.

"Right, come on, back to the trailer. We have a race to prepare for!"

Chapter 10
Our time

Adam was now beginning to get nervous and worried that Damson had worn herself out charging around the show wildly.

"We're bound to come last," he whimpered.

"Now that's not the spirit, is it? Remember we have a Best Exhibit donkey on our hands here," said Mum encouragingly.

Then dear little Noah had one of those moments he seemed to have when, out of the blue, he said exactly the right thing.

"I just know you're going to do well and if you don't win, I'll still love you both."

No one could speak and tried to look busy so they didn't cry.

Poppy checked over Damson's reins and told Adam he looked spectacular in his racing silks, which made him feel much better. Mum kept whispering into Damson's ear.

"Do your best, girl. Bring Adam home safely and run like the wind."

Agnes let out a loud bleat from the trailer as if to say "Go, girl."

Then there was an announcement over the public address system.

"Would all Donkey Derby entrants proceed to the main ring collecting area, please."

Adam's heart pounded like it had never done before and his mouth dried. He mounted Damson and gently stroked her neck.

"This is it, girl. Our moment. Just do your best," he said gently.

Damson's ears pricked up and he knew she was listening and ready.

When they arrived at the collecting area, even Mum's and Dad's hearts began to thump. Eighteen other donkeys were circling round and round. Dad let go of the reins, said a final "Go for it!" and patted Damson's rump.

Adam joined the circle of donkeys. He couldn't believe how big some of them looked and their jockeys had that confident smirk of "Try and beat me then."

One girl jockey swaggered alongside him.

"First time?" she called out.

"Yes," Adam mumbled back.

"I'd stay at the back, out of trouble, if I were you. It can get rough out there," she warned.

Another freckly boy on a black donkey called Sooty informed Adam that he'd won the Derby for the last two years and wasn't about to give up the cup. Adam got more and more nervous.

Damson, on the other hand, didn't look anxious at all. In fact, she was loving meeting all these other donkeys. There was Sammy, Doughnut, Pip, Randolph, Georgie, Ivor and Trooper. The ones Adam feared most were named Flash and Lightning.

Mum decided that Adam's racing silks were without doubt the smartest and she was really pleased with her efforts. Several riders looked almost scruffy.

"Just look at that rider. Don't they know that pink and orange clash?" she sneered.

"Stop it," said Dad.

Mr Jackson from the sanctuary arrived and shouted good luck to Adam. He had been checking all the donkeys were healthy and fit.

Poppy and Noah were thrilled when the show president insisted the family all come and take seats in the main stand. They had the best view of the arena ever and got free pop and nibbles. One by one, the donkeys were announced and then paraded to the start line. When Damson was called out, the whole arena went wild. People stood, cameras flashed and the press photographers all tried to get a shot of her. Adam glowed, Mum and Dad and the children cried and Damson trotted at her best.

The other riders were furious that she got such a reception, especially the boy on Sooty, who made a miserable face.

The donkeys lined up, the crowd silenced and the starter slowly raised his flag. The riders gripped their reins tightly, holding back their donkeys who were desperate to get started. When the flag finally fell, it became obvious not all were that desperate. Two refused to move, one turned round and went backwards and another walked off so slowly he was left behind in seconds.

Damson made a good start and stayed just behind the three leaders – Randolph, Trixie and, of course, Sooty. There was lots of shouting, clicking and screaming amongst the jockeys.

"Go, go!"

"Wow, wow, wow!"

"Get on!"

But Adam sat tightly and gently encouraged Damson by whispering "Good girl."

After the first lap of three, Damson fell back to fifth as Doughnut overtook her. Some of the jockeys were kicking a bit too hard for Adam's liking and waving reins wildly.

He held his nerve and
kept Damson at a good
canter. On lap two,
Randolph took too
sharp a turn and his
rider tumbled off.
Thankfully the grass
was nice and soft.
Then Trixie and
Doughnut saw the
way out of the ring

and, despite all the efforts
of their jockeys to stop them, headed for the
hay. This meant Damson was now in second
place, but then a donkey called Candyfloss
levelled alongside her. Sooty was still in front.

Then something extraordinary happened.
The crowd began to shout.

"Damson! Damson! Go, go, Damson!"

Soon the whole arena was chanting
Damson's name.

Adam whispered, "This is it, Damson. It's
our time."

Damson somehow knew and responded to Adam and the crowd.

On the last bend, she cut inside Sooty and galloped at top speed down the final straight, winning by half a length. The crowd went wild, Poppy screamed till her throat was sore and Noah kept saying, "I told you so, I told you so."

Mum and Dad hugged and hugged and tears were running down their cheeks.

Damson did a victory lap and the boy on Sooty just about managed to say, "Well done"

in a mumbled grunt. Then added, "Wait till next year," in a way that was quite unsporting.

The crowd just went wild and the family joined Adam in the main arena for the presentation.

The cup was presented by Mr Jackson, which made it so special, and Damson got a blue sash this time with the words Derby Champion printed on it in gold letters.

She also got a voucher for a year's supply of barley straw and hay, which was a great help to the family's finances.

After press photos and lots of patting again, they loaded Damson into the trailer. Agnes was really excited to see them back at last and nuzzled Damson. The people in the 'shiny monster' were loading their horses too.

"How did you do?" asked Mum.

"Won fourth place in the over-14 hands novice jumping," one replied.

"Oh," went Mum walking off, waving the Derby trophy in the air deliberately, with a big smirk on her face!

Chapter 11
Damson Day

On the Monday that followed, Damson received a hero's welcome at the children's school. Mr Milner the headteacher had heard about Damson's derby victory and asked the children's mum and dad to bring her in for the children to celebrate. By the time Mum and Dad drew up at the gates at 11am, the whole school had been busy preparing.

One class had made donkey-shaped bunting, another flags to wave with donkey drawings on them and the oldest class had made banners with the words 'We love Damson!', 'Go, Damson, go!', 'Damson the Derby Dasher!' and 'Damson faster than lightning'.

The three Greenwood children had been given permission to come into school later than usual so they could lead Damson onto the playground. They had made her look her very best with her bridle and saddle polished till they sparkled and with her blue derby winner sash on. Dad had put polish on her hooves too, and Mum had trimmed the end of her tail hairs!

Poppy and Noah led Damson in and Adam walked beside them holding the Derby Trophy Cup above his head. He wore his racing silks, which Mum had washed and ironed to perfection.

The school children formed two long lines and waved and cheered wildly as Damson and the children paraded between them, loving every moment.

All the teachers and classroom assistants were there too, and even the kitchen staff came out and cheered and waved tea towels in the air.

Lots of parents came back to school, as they wanted to add their congratulations.

Mrs Dodds the lollipop lady stood right at the back, waving her lollipop sign as she was still nervous after being chased.

Mr Milner had phoned the local press and, to everyone's surprise and the children's delight, a TV crew arrived.

After lots of filming and photos, patting and taking turns to lead Damson, Mr Milner called for quiet. He then made a wonderful speech saying how proud he was of the Greenwood family and their amazing donkey Damson. He then went on to say, "In recognition of this wonderful achievement, the nearest school day to July 5th will always be known as Damson Day." The children cheered, even though they didn't really know what a Damson Day was. "And on this day every year we'll have a school picnic on the field, to which Damson will be invited."

The children cheered even more.

Unknown to the children, Mr Milner had already asked the cooks to prepare a picnic instead of hot school dinners.

It was a wonderful occasion with jam and chocolate spread sandwiches, gorgeous cupcakes with chocolate flakes and Smarties on, crisps, bananas, sausage rolls and lemonade.

Damson was given four large carrots and then grazed merrily as the children ate.

After an extra long lunchtime with time to play rounders, football, netball and cricket, the children returned to their classes.

For the rest of the afternoon they were all asked to 'celebrate' donkeys. Some children painted or drew a donkey, others wrote poems and stories.

Poppy and Adam's class made models from modelling clay and four children did some research on the computer and discovered amazing donkey facts:

- There are around 42 million donkeys in the world today.
- There are approximately 170 different breeds.
- Donkeys live to between 30 and 40 years old.
- Around 900 donkeys work giving seaside rides.
- China has more donkeys than any other country in the world.

At 3pm, Damson was loaded back into the trailer and the children waved goodbye through their classroom windows. Noah, Adam and Poppy were totally exhausted and fell asleep in the car before reaching home.

That night they all slept well, and had wonderful dreams about one of the best days ever!

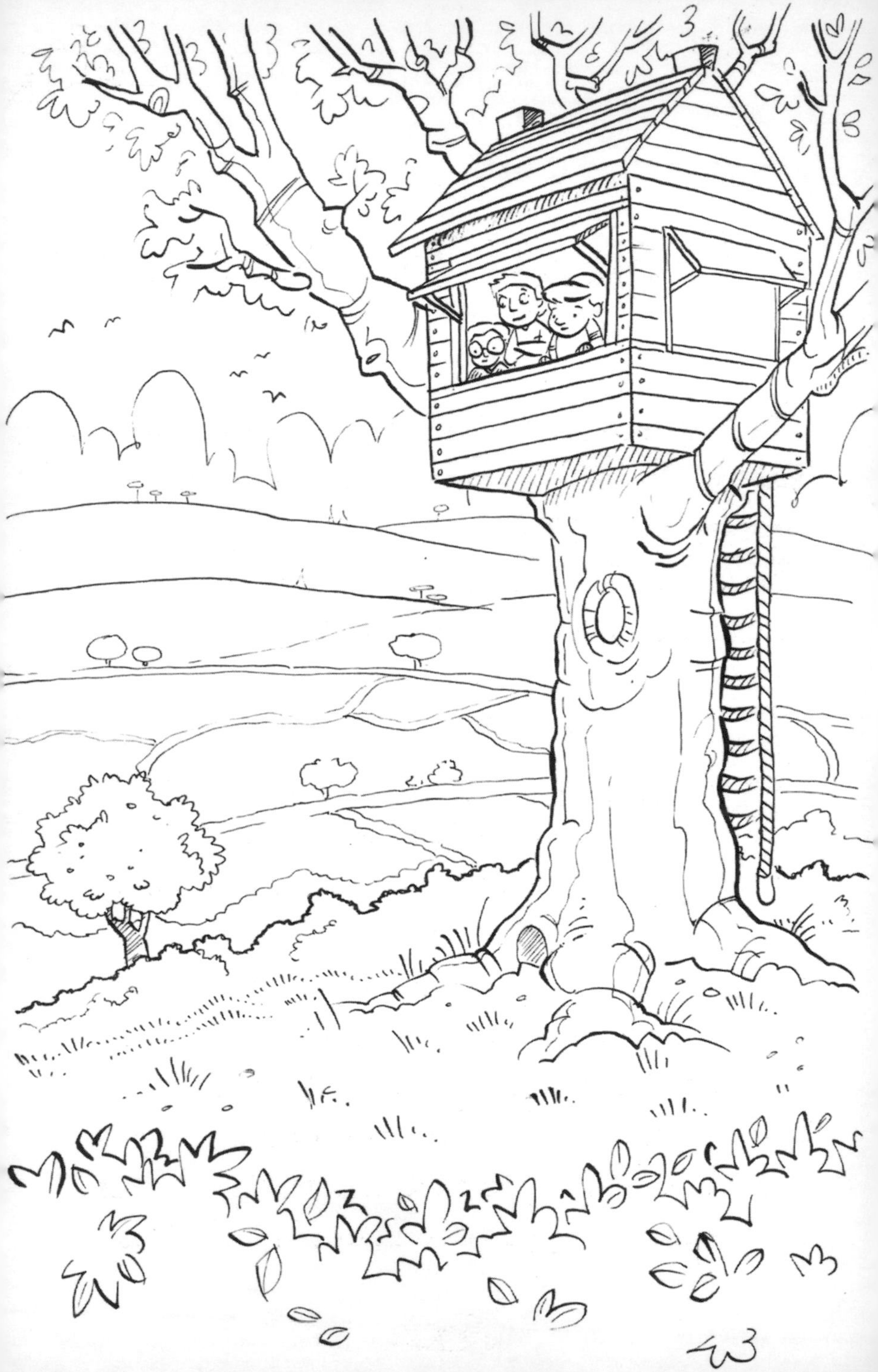

Chapter 12
A star is born

Life began to settle down again during the summer holidays. The children spent most of their days in the orchard keeping Damson and Agnes company. The geese continued to wander in and out and Dad helped the children make a treehouse in the tallest apple tree. They called it The Damson Lookout Den. From there they could watch their beloved Damson as she nibbled her way around the orchard, and see the whole of the farm. They could also see beyond their home, down the valley with its ever-changing shades of green and the small woodland clumps on its slopes that the children sometimes walked to. It made them realise just how lucky they were.

Even Noah felt the need to say, "Sometimes I think no one else lives on our planet but us!"

The other two were too surprised to answer.

It was a lovely long summer with long days too, as Damson always woke the children at 7am by braying endlessly like a donkey alarm clock until they drew back the curtains and, through an open window, shouted, "OK, we're up!"

In August, they were visited by the vet who said Damson was in perfect condition and congratulated the family for the care they were giving her. She also clipped her hooves as they were getting a little long and gave Mum some worming medication to stop her getting worms.

The children liked Sandy the vet as she was always smiling and very gentle. It was during that month that Damson also did several of her 'amazing escape' stunts. On three occasions she was nowhere to be seen and yet again it was a mystery how she got out. On two of the 'escapes', she was found nibbling away in fields in the lower valley and on the other she actually brought herself back home!

As autumn arrived, Damson began to spend more time in the lower barn as it began to get damper and colder outside. In mid-December, the first snow fell and Damson was let out for a short time to have fun with the children. At first she didn't quite know what to make of it and trotted about as if walking on fire. But once she saw the children having fun rolling in it, she decided to copy them and lay down and rolled and rolled! The children even made her a snow donkey!

As Christmas drew closer, Damson made her first stage appearance! Mr Milner had asked Mum and Dad if she could be in the school nativity play. After a bit of thought, they agreed. Much to the children's delight, Damson was to carry Mary into Bethlehem and then stand in the stable where Jesus was born. As Adam had been chosen as Joseph, they felt sure she would behave, as it was him who was to lead her in.

The dress rehearsal went quite well, although there was an upset when two children playing sheep had to sit for so long on stage they wet themselves. Mrs Clarke, a mum helper, got a mop and helped the children do a 'quick change'!

They also discovered that Freddie Ashford was allergic to straw and hay and sneezed so much that they had to swap him from being a shepherd to the innkeeper's son.

Damson walked in perfectly with Nicki Nutall onboard as Mary and then stood at the bottom of the stage quietly next to six rats and three frogs (played by members of the reception and Year 1 classes!).

On the night of the real performance, Damson was kept in her trailer until the last moment to keep her calm.

The school hall was packed with parents who were already holding tissues, as they knew they'd cry, as they always did!

There had been one last-minute panic when Martin Aspinall's mum phoned in saying he had been really sick and couldn't come in for the performance.

However, Colin Thornbury, one of the most able boys in the school with an amazing memory, said he knew all Martin's lines, so he stepped in!

The lights in the hall went down and the narrator began. "Over 2,000 years ago, when Herod was King of Judea..."

Adam then waited for his cue.

"Joseph brought Mary slowly to Bethlehem on a donkey as she was having a baby..."

At this point, Adam and Damson entered

the hall through the fire exit at the back. Everyone went "Aaah".

However, someone had put the spotlight at a funny angle and it was shining into Adam's and Damson's eyes. Neither could see where they were going and instead of heading towards the stage, they ended up in the PE cupboard!

With some help from Mr Ovens, who grabbed Adam's hand, they walked to the stage and positioned themselves safely there.

Damson stood looking almost angelic, along with the other characters on stage! Yes, she did begin to eat Baby Jesus's manger straw, but no one minded as the donkey probably did on the real day when Jesus was born!

So Damson was a star, as ever!

Chapter 13
The surprise!

During the spring months, Damson returned to the blossom-filled orchard when it was warm enough.

The children enjoyed their usual Easter Egg Hunt with Dad hiding behind trees with bunny ears on. It was Poppy who made the first comment as she ate a large chunk of Easter egg.

"I'm glad we haven't got any chocolate for Damson, just a carrot, as her tummy is getting a bit fat!"

"You know you're right," agreed Mum.

"Perhaps we're letting her graze a little too much on that spring grass," said Adam.

"No, I'm keeping a careful eye on how long she's out in the orchard," replied Dad.

It took a moment for the penny to drop, as they say, but it was good old Noah who blurted it out.

"Has she got a baby in her tummy like Mary had with Jesus?"

Dad began to say, "Don't be so daft..." But he suddenly stopped.

"What about all those times she escaped?" he questioned. "She might have...", but he stopped again.

Then pandemonium broke out. Everyone was talking at the same time and no one would stop.

Mum finally shouted at the top of her voice.

"Stop it! We might all be getting excited for nothing. Now let's calm down and give Sandy the vet a ring," she said calmly.

By a bit of luck, Sandy was at the next farm about a mile away and said she would call in after treating a horse that had cut its leg on a fence.

The children were ordered to go and sit in the treehouse, out of the way. They did as they were told, but very grumpily.

From there they could see Sandy had

brought a kind of hand scanner with her and was rubbing it along Damson's tummy.

Then they saw what they had been praying for. Sandy nodded!

The children leapt from the treehouse and hurtled towards them. Sandy, Mum and Dad were grinning from ear to ear.

"Yes, she's pregnant!" announced Sandy.

Adam ran round and round the orchard. Poppy did cartwheels across the front lawn and Noah just rolled around the ground getting very muddy.

Once things finally calmed down, Sandy spent some time explaining things, over a cup of tea and a chocolate digestive.

Adam got a pad and wrote everything down, as he wanted to be really prepared.

She told them that she thought the baby was around eight months and so it should be August when the foal would be born as it usually took from 11 to 12 months.

They were told that they could begin to give Damson a little more food now to help feed the baby inside her, and only gentle exercise.

They were also told that Damson might sometimes want to be on her own with some peace and quiet.

The children proved to be the perfect donkey-carers and spent lots of time in the treehouse just watching and, of course, waiting. They also kept the children at school informed, as there had been great excitement at the news.

One class had a tick chart showing the days to the expected birth.

On the last day of the summer term, the

children promised they would let all their friends know when the foal was born.

The three children had been waiting for so long that when the actual day arrived, they were caught off-guard. Adam was mucking out Milly while Poppy and Noah were feeding the rabbits. They hadn't noticed Damson making her way slowly to the back of the orchard.

It was several hours before Dad said, "Where's Damson?" They looked in the barn. She wasn't there and, at first, couldn't be seen in the orchard.

The children went and got Mum and were told to follow Dad quietly around the orchard.

Then, just like the first day, they found Damson. Two unmistakable ears could be seen pointing above the tall grass.

As they got closer, there lying next to Damson was a beautiful little brown foal.

Damson was licking it all over as it had only just been born and was covered in sticky goo, as Noah called it.

The family sat down gently and just talked to Damson.

"Well done, Damson. Good girl," said Dad softly.

"And all by yourself, you clever mum," said Mum proudly.

"Hello, mummy and baby," whispered Poppy.

"What a girl," sighed Adam.

Little Noah then chose just the right words yet again.

"We love you loads, Damson," he announced.

They then left Damson alone as Sandy had recommended, but kept watch from the treehouse.

Mum and Dad took it in turns to check things were going well. Finally, the little foal stood up and made its first steps. Dad whispered, "It's a little boy."

Adam then suddenly remembered they had promised to let everyone know when the foal was born.

They hurried indoors and got paper and felt-tip pens to make posters to put around the village.

"But what shall we call him?" asked Poppy.

"Good question," said Mum.

They all thought and then, yes, good old Noah said, "Apple, as he was born under an apple tree."

Everyone gave him the biggest hug they had ever given him (which got on his nerves).

The family then set off into the village to put the posters up announcing the birth of Baby Apple.

But you know, one mystery was never solved. They never did find out where Damson had come from or how she managed to get in and out of the orchard!

NEIL GRIFFITHS lives in the cottage of his
dreams in a small village in Wiltshire. It's
his 'secret hideaway', that overlooks fields
that echo to the sounds of sheep, cattle and
a yet-to-be-spotted spring cuckoo! Neil
loves animals, but due to his work taking
him all over the world, he doesn't have any
of his own. Yet!

Find out more about Neil here:
www.cornertolearn.co.uk

JANETTE LOUDEN is an 'English lady'
living abroad, in America! She has
illustrated a number of Neil's books and
shares his passion for all things furry!

Find out more about Janette here:
www.janettelouden.com

THE DONKEY SANCTUARY

Over 50 million donkeys and mules exist in the world. Many need care and protection from a life of suffering and neglect, while others have a vital role to play in human survival and happiness. These gentle, affectionate creatures are at the heart of everything The Donkey Sanctuary does.

Founded in 1969 by Dr Elisabeth Svendsen MBE, The Donkey Sanctuary is an international charity that provides sanctuary to neglected and abandoned donkeys and mules and works to improve donkey welfare in many countries around the world.

The Donkey Sanctuary has 10 sanctuaries around the UK and Europe that provide lifelong care to almost 7,000 donkeys and mules. It also operates in many countries around the world, including Mexico, Peru, Egypt,

Ethiopia, Romania, Portugal and India. It is collaborative in all its activities, working through a network of partner organisations, individuals and communities.

Its vision is a world where donkeys and mules live free from suffering and their

contribution to humanity is fully valued. Its mission is to transform the quality of life for donkeys, mules and people worldwide through greater understanding, collaboration and support, and by promoting lasting, mutually life-enhancing relationships.

Its work is funded entirely by donations and legacy gifts. If you would like to make a donation to the charity or adopt a donkey, visit the website and find out more:

www.thedonkeysanctuary.org.uk

Why not visit The Donkey Sanctuary at its international headquarters in Sidmouth, Devon, where you can meet some of the 500 donkeys currently in its care!

Look out for...

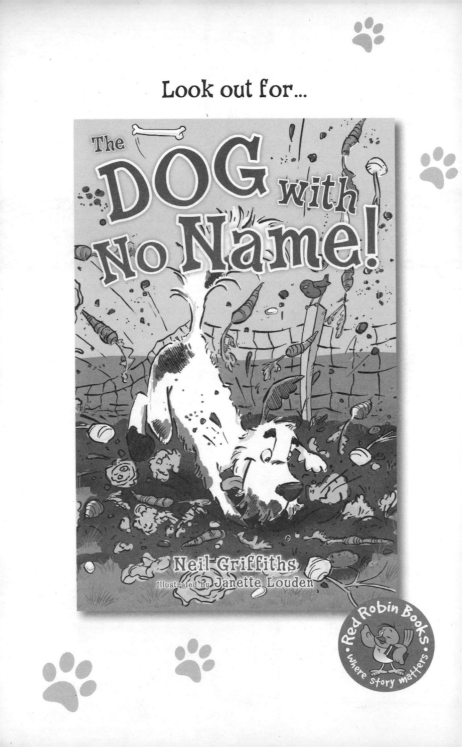

The **DOG** with **No Name!**

Neil Griffiths

Illustrated By Janette Louden

Red Robin Books
· where story matters ·